Ms. Blue knows one pumpkin song.
On our bus trip home, we sing along.

Twenty pumpkin pies on the wall.
Twenty pumpkin pies.
Take one down, pass it around.
Nineteen pumpkin pies on the wall...

Nineteen pumpkin pies on the wall...
Nineteen pumpkin pies.
Take one down, pass it around.
Eighteen pumpkin pies on the wall...

"Here's our bus again," says Gwen.
"Buddies line up two by two," says Drew.
"Back to school we go," says Ignacio.

"Three bites.
Bye, pumpkin pie!"
says Di.

"Five tables,
times four
snacks,"
says Max.

Six pumpkins, green and white.

6

Lots that are just right!

"Eight orange pumpkins, tall," says Paul.

Seven yellow pumpkins, bumpy.

"Wow! Pumpkins everywhere!"
shouts Claire.

"It's picking time in the pumpkin patch!"
calls Farmer Mixenmatch.

"Yay! A tractor ride," says Clyde.

"We sit nine on each side."

"Plus two in the back," says Zack.

"This way!" calls Mei.
"Come on," calls Shawn.

"This maze has ten scarecrows," says Rose.

"Dead end. Uh-oh!" calls Ignacio.

"Eleven bees are making honey!" says Sunny.

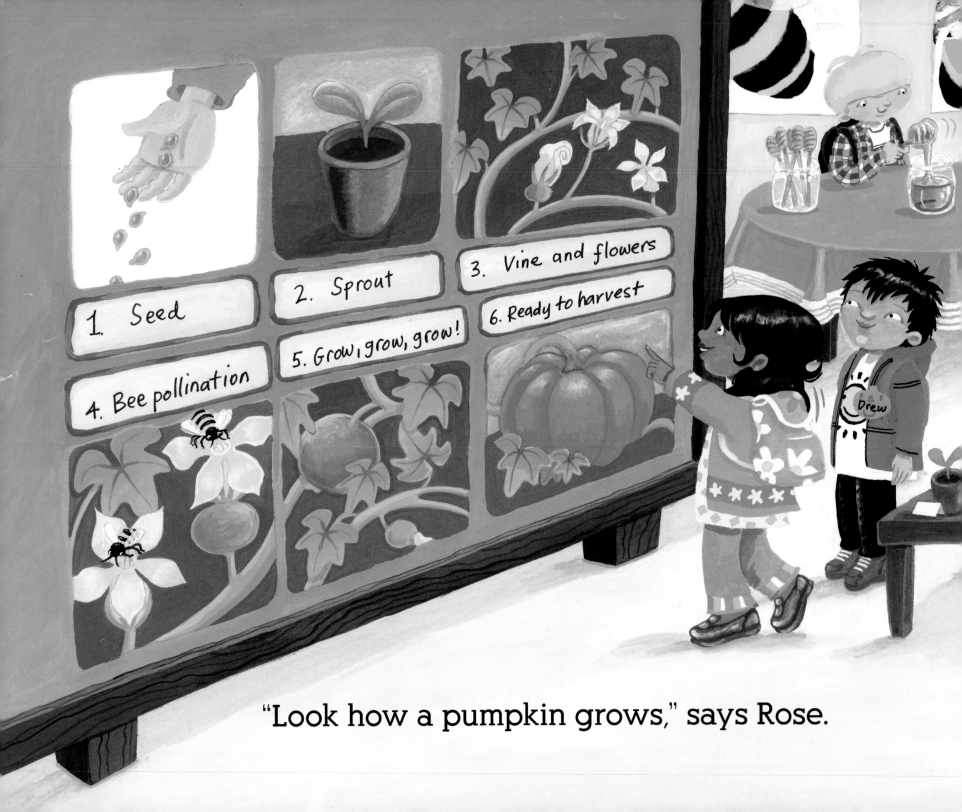

"Look how a pumpkin grows," says Rose.

"The bunny hopped away!" says Mei.

"But a pony galloped in," says Gwen.

"Still twelve pets in the zoo!" counts Drew.

"Twelve pets in the petting zoo," says Drew.

"Six chicks—four yellow, two black," says Zack.

"Three pigs—two big, one small," says Paul.

"Two goats and one bunny," says Sunny.

"Welcome to my pumpkin patch!"
calls Farmer Mixenmatch.

"**Thirteen** pumpkins point the way," says Mei.

"Fourteen cars got here before us," says Russ.

"I hope the pumpkins aren't all gone," says Shawn.

"Look! Fifteen Pumpkin Street," reads Pete.

"Guess sixteen things we'll see
on our field trip today," says Mei.

"I spy seventeen orange things that are not your name tags. Can you spy them all?" asks Paul.

"Now all ten seats have two," says Drew.

"Okay! We can go!" shouts Ignacio.

"Eighteen kids get on our bus," says Russ.

"But someone's late," says Kate.

"Wait for me!" calls Kiri.

"For nineteen kids plus Ms. Blue," says Drew.

"There are twenty name tags to make," says Jake.

"It's our pumpkin patch field trip!" shouts Chip.

"Yippee!" says Kiri.

"Woo-hoo!" says Drew.